Jace Stone

CONTENTS

Content Warning:

Ask Me Nicely may contain triggers for some people. Contains explicit language, forced (forced fantasy) sex, and stranger sex. Reader discretion is advised.

ISBN-13: 978-1542552974

ISBN-10: 1542552974

Ask Me Nicely

Dark Urges, Book 1

Facebook.com/authorjacestone

Cover by Anya Kelleye Designs

Jace Stone

Ask Me Nicely

Dark Urges, Book 1

Acknowledgments

Lisa Angel Miller, Editor and formatter...

Thank you for always being available to go over plots, brainstorm scenes, and for your never-ending support and encouragement. The list is way too long to write out, but thank you for everything.

There was something else...what was it? Oh, thanks for making it pretty.

Anya Kelleye, Cover Design...

You never cease to amaze me with your creativity and ability to always get it right.

Thank you so much.

My street team...

Thank you so much for everything you do for me. Your tireless promotion day in and day out is greatly appreciated.

Chapter 1

The bass thumping from the loud speakers vibrated in his chest, which only added to the excitement he was feeling. The adrenaline rush, the unknown, the game, moving in for the kill to seal the deal...it was all exhilarating. He nodded but ignored his best friend and coworker, who was trying to shout over the music. Tommy Reid kept his eyes glued to the sea of swaying hips that greeted him on the dance floor. The One Night Stand was the most happening club in the Tampa Bay area. Lucky for him, he knew the doorman and was able to gain entrance.

"Rum and coke," he shouted to the bartender and then turned his back against the bar.

"Can you feel that, Jeremy? Tonight's the night, man. I can feel it."

"Oh yeah, buddy, I feel it all right." Jeremy hooked his left arm around Tommy's neck in a fake headlock. "But we both know we're going home alone again, so don't get your hopes up. Okay?"

"Get the fuck off me, man." Tommy ripped Jeremy's arm from around his neck. "People are going to think we're a couple or something. And you're wrong. Tonight's the night."

"Sure, man. Let's drink up and enjoy the show, okay? I got next round." Jeremy settled against the bar, watching his buddy from the corner of his eye. *Motherfucker sure seems on edge tonight.*

Tommy straightened up off the bar and took a small step forward, his eyes locked on something or someone out on the dance floor.

Oh shit, here we go. Jeremy watched his friend. "See something you like?"

"Black mini skirt wrapped around a thick ass and thick legs that run clean up to that beautiful work of art." Tommy never took his eyes off the brunette who had caught his attention.

"Shit, Tommy boy, that's half the girls on the dance floor. Which one's got you all hot and bothered?"

"Blue shirt, dancing with the blonde in the green pantsuit, two o' clock."

Jeremy scanned the sea of bodies until he located the objects of Tommy's newfound obsession. "Oh shit, Tommy boy, you've set your sights high tonight, my man."

Tommy snapped his head around and glared at his buddy. "Are you trying to say something?"

"Easy, man." Jeremy raised both hands. "I'm on your side here. I think you're the nicest and coolest guy around. But girls like that don't date guys like us."

"Guys like us?" He turned full on to face his friend. "You mean guys who have a steady job and handle their responsibilities? Guys who want nothing more than to love and be loved by someone who's willing to go all in and give as good as they get?" Tommy pointed toward the dancefloor. "Girls like that would be lucky to have guys like us. It's guys like us who pay attention and do our damndest to meet every single fucking need."

Jeremy stared at his best friend, completely taken back by the display of anger. "Look, bro, I get it and I agree. But girls like that only date guys who are built like Greek gods, have ten-inch dicks, and a shit load of money." He reached forward and grabbed

Tommy's shoulder. "I haven't ever seen your dick, but I do know you aren't rich and the both of us could stand to lose fifteen pounds or so." Jeremy grabbed his drink off the bar. "C'mon, man. It's been a hell of a week, so let's drink up."

Tommy finished off the contents of his glass and placed it on the bar before looking down at the slight pudge that hung over his belt. At six-foot-one, he carried his two hundred and three pounds well. Construction helped keep him in decent shape and he was far from fat, but still not sporting a gym rat body either.

"You good, man?" Jeremy's voice brought him out of the self-evaluation he had slipped off into.

"Hell yeah, bro." Tommy flashed a big smile and slapped his buddy on the arm. "I'm about to go show these girls what they're missing out on."

"Tommy, wait! Damn it, Tommy!" Jeremy shouted to the back of his friend as he stepped out onto the dance floor, making a beeline for the two chicks of their earlier conversation.

Every weekend it was the same ole story. Give him an A for effort though; he wasn't scared to try. He'd talk to anybody and try his best to pick up the hottest women in the bar. It always ended the same though. They went home alone. Tommy really was a great guy. He'd give anybody the shirt off his back. But, so many women had fucked him over, he was a little jaded at times.

Tommy slid up in front of Black Mini Skirt in what appeared to be half electric slide and half robot. "Good evening. I'm Tommy." He flashed his biggest smile. "How are you ladies tonight?"

Mini Skirt rolled her eyes, turned her back to him, and continued to dance with her friend. The dim room and flashing strobe lights hid the red as it creeped up Tommy's neck and onto his face. He looked around the room, but the fact that nobody was paying him any attention did nothing to lessen the embarrassment he was feeling.

Tommy stepped forward and placed his hand in the middle of her back. "Hey, I was hoping—"

Mini Skirt spun on a dime and brushed away his hand. "—Why are you touching me?"

"Oh, hold on now." He pulled his hand back. "I didn't mean anything by it. I was just trying to get your attention."

"Well, don't!" She started bouncing to the rhythm of the music again.

"Okay, cool. You don't like to be touched." Tommy forced a smile he didn't feel. "Hey, I'm not very good at dancing to this stuff, but I was hoping maybe it would be okay if I asked you to dance the next slow song?"

He watched her eyes as she looked him over from head to toe before she burst out laughing. "You can't be serious? Do you really think I would dance with you?" She cocked her head back toward Pantsuit and cut her eyes back to Tommy. "Help me out, Marie. I can't tell. Are those Walmart brand clothes or are you thinking his mom made them for him?"

Marie's laughter could be heard above the music. "Oh c'mon, Amy, you're losing your touch. Clearly, those are straight off the Goodwill clearance rack."

The girls gave each other a high five before Amy turned her attention back to Tommy. "Just go away, will ya?"

Tommy made his way back to the bar where Jeremy was waiting for him with a fresh drink.

"How'd it go, buddy?"

"She practically begged for my number." He winked and grabbed his drink. "I'm calling it a night after this one."

"Yeah, I'm ready too, man." Jeremy grinned and gave a knowing nod. "I was about to leave when I saw you headed back over here."

"Go ahead and take off, man. I'm going to pay the tab and head out." Tommy reached out and shook Jeremy's hand. "I'll holler at you tomorrow, bro."

Tommy paid the tab and left his half-full glass on the bar. He took a deep breath and headed back across the dance floor to Amy and Marie. The girls were both dancing and grinding with two pretty boys in expensive suits and too busy to notice his approach. He stopped just behind Amy and tapped her on the shoulder. "Excuse me?"

She turned to face him, the disdain evident on her face. "I thought I told you to go away!" she hissed.

Tommy smiled sweetly and leaned in close to her ear. “You should have asked me nicely.”

Chapter 2

Tommy sat in the red Toyota Tundra and replayed the events of the night over and over, trying to figure out where he'd went wrong.

I can't be that bad of a guy, damn it. Maybe not rich and maybe not a ripped-up muscle head, but damn.

He hated that there were so called stations or classes of people. Tommy ran his fingers through his hair and let out the deep breath he hadn't realized he was holding.

"Her loss," he muttered and slid down in the seat of his truck. He hadn't had a cigarette in almost seven months, but he found himself craving one now. The waiting, the boredom of staring at the door, was grating on his nerves.

"Son of a bitch. What the fuck is taking so long?" he mumbled to the empty truck cab as he glanced at the clock on the radio. Two-twenty-one. Though he'd only been waiting for just over an hour, it felt like an eternity.

I'm really a nice guy. A simple "no thank you" would have sufficed. And what the hell is wrong with my clothes? Maybe not name brand, but not hand-me-down either. Tommy laid his head back against the seat and raked his face with his hand. *Don't go there. Don't head down that path. Not now...*

Tommy grabbed the half-dozen roses from the seat beside him and exited the truck. He all but ran to the front door. He couldn't wait to see the look on Nicole's face when she realized that not only was he home early, but he was taking her away for the weekend. She had been hinting at and talking about how nice it would be to spend a few days away relaxing on a beach somewhere. He eased the front door open and quietly stepped inside, already picturing the huge smile that was going to spread across her face; the smile that was responsible for completely melting him every single time he saw it. Tommy tiptoed up the stairs to the master bedroom and ever so gently turned the doorknob. Careful not to make any noise, he slowly pushed open the door.

"Nicole? Honey, I'm home and I have surprise for you."

Tommy's eyes locked on his lovely wife's. She stared back in total shock and disbelief from their bed as she let the stranger's cock fall from her mouth.

"What the fuck is going on here, Nicole?"

The strange man brushed Nicole to the side and off his body. "Look, man." He jumped out of the bed and grabbed his pants from the floor. "I don't want any trouble, I thought—"

"—Shut the fuck up," Tommy hissed. "Open your mouth again and I'll kill you." He took a step toward the bed and pointed the flowers back at the door. "Just get the fuck out before you get hurt."

Tommy turned his attention back to his wife as the half-naked man slid past him and out the door.

"I don't..." He turned around and sat on the foot of the bed. "I don't understand...why?"

Nicole leapt from the bed and rushed around in front of Tommy. "Really? You don't understand why?" she sneered. "You're a nobody, Tommy. My father was right. I never should have married you." She reached for her clothes on the foot of the bed and snatched them from beneath her husband's ass. "I'm a beautiful woman, Tommy. I deserve a man with a nice body. A man who dresses better than you. A man with enough money to give me the things I deserve. A man I can be proud of." She ran to the bedroom door then stopped and turned to him again. "He's all of those things. He's the man you'll never be."

"Baby, wait up!" Nicole shouted as she practically ran down the stairs. "I'm coming with you. Fuck this loser..."

Tommy sat up straight in the truck seat and relaxed his jaw, easing the ache. *Why do you always have to go back there and remember that shit? Forget that whoring bitch.* He pinched the bridge of his nose and sighed. *Damn, I want a cigarette.*

"Fuck it," he said aloud and reached for the gear shift. With one last glance at the door, he dropped the truck into drive.

Shit, there they are!

Chapter 3

Tommy killed the lights before easing the big Toyota up on the curb. It had been an hour since he had followed the little blue BMW home. Seeing them both enter the house had almost deterred him. But spending what felt like eternity circling the block had given him enough time to devise a plan. Now that the lights were out, it was time to put that plan into action.

Tommy exited the truck and eased the door shut before making his way across the street and up the front lawn. With two pieces of wire from his tool box, he put the skills he had learned as a teenager to use on the cheap door lock. The lock clicking sounded loud on the night's still air as it announced its retraction into the door. He inhaled deeply and slowly let it out before gently pushing the door open just enough for him to slide past it and into the house. His ears picked up the heavy snoring long before his eyes adjusted to the darkness. The numbers on the DVD player clock cast a green glow across the couch where the sleeping woman lay. Tommy took one last deep breath to steady his nerves before removing his shoes. The tile floor was cool beneath his socked feet as he slowly made his way over to the couch. The blonde hair that had been so perfectly in place just a few hours before now resembled an abandoned rat's nest lying on top of the pillow. Marie's drunken snores spoke volumes about the depth of her sleep and just how easy this was going to be.

Ignoring her for a moment, Tommy softly made his way toward the hallway. With limited vision, his sense of hearing was working overtime trying to find the real reason he was here. The painted wood was cool to his face as he pressed his ear against the door. His breathing seemed overly loud in the quiet hallway. The doorknob turned beneath his hand and he gently pushed open the door. It moaned on its hinges. Blind panic ripped through his body and he froze. After what seemed like an eternity, he slowly let out the breath he had been holding. The obnoxious snores coming from the living room was music to his ears. Tommy lifted on the doorknob to ease the weight on the hinges and pushed the door open enough to slide his head through. A damned bathroom. Rather than take any more chances, he left the bathroom door open and slowly made his way down the hall. Only one door left. This one had to be the one. Just on the other side of that door was the woman who couldn't settle for just rejecting him. No, she had to try to humiliate him. Nervous excitement in the form of an adrenaline rush raced through his veins. All he wanted to do was dance and talk a little. A simple *no thank you* would have worked just fine.

Tommy inhaled deeply and slowly let the air escape through his nose. Two more slow, deep breaths to steady his nerves and he reached for the doorknob to what had to be the master suite. His senses now in overdrive, his nerve endings on fire, he slowly pushed the door open.

The half-moon peeked through sheer white curtains and cast a serene glow throughout the room. It was almost romantic. The nightstand in the corner held an upside-down novel with a half-naked couple on the cover. A thin throw hung over the back of the rocking chair next to the nightstand. Her dark brown hair glistened from the moonlight and was a perfect contrast to the solid white pillowcase. Her even breathing could not be heard from across the room but was evident by the slight but steady rise and fall of her breasts beneath the comforter. Everything about this room and woman was picture perfect. Almost involuntarily, Tommy tiptoed over to the side of the bed, his eyes still locked on the beauty lying beneath the covers. It was hard to believe that someone who possessed such physical beauty could be so damned ugly on the inside. The memory of the incident at the club snapped him back to reality and the reason he was here.

The fact that she was lying completely beneath the covers with only her head sticking out was making this easier than it was supposed to be. Tommy swung one leg over her sleeping body and straddled her. His knees pinned the comforter to the bed and her arms beneath it. As soon as his weight settled on the bed, he leaned forward, applying most of his body weight to hers, and clamped his left hand over her mouth.

Amy's eyes shot open and panic flashed through them. Her scream was muffled by his hand and her whole body jerked beneath his weight as she tried to free herself.

"Shhh. I'm not going to hurt you. But you have to stop fighting. Okay?"

She screamed again and fought him harder, but her smaller size was no match for the two hundred pounds of dead weight on top of her.

Tommy placed his forehead against hers and growled, “Shut up. Do it now.”

The harsh, no nonsense tone got her attention. Wide, fear-filled eyes met his as her body went rigid beneath him.

“Look, I know you’re frightened.” He intentionally kept his voice soft. “But I’m not going to hurt you. I promise. But you have to stay still, and you have to be quiet.”

Amy’s body didn’t relax any at all, but she stopped trying to scream out through her covered mouth.

Tommy sat up and looked around the room, still holding his hand clamped over her mouth. His eyes settled on the extra pillow beside her.

“Okay, listen to me,” he said. “I’m going to take the pillowcase off that pillow and gag you with it. Just until I know you won’t scream.” Tommy laid the duct tape he’d retrieved from his toolbox on the bed beside her head and reached for the pillow. “I’ll be as gentle as possible, so don't fight me and make this harder than it has to be."

He stripped the pillow off the pillowcase and replaced his hand with it over her mouth. "I'm going to wrap it around the back of your head so the tape doesn't stick to your hair."

Tommy slid his free hand beneath her head and gently lifted it from the pillow. He wrapped the tape around her face, over the top of the pillowcase, and sat up straight. "See? That wasn't so bad now, was it?"

He pulled his shirt over his head and laid it on her chest. The look of pure panic suddenly returned to her eyes. "Relax," he chuckled. "I'm just going to use it to wrap your wrists in the same way I used the pillowcase on your face." Tommy shifted his weight to his left side and fished her arm from beneath the covers and his right leg. Leaning to the right, he repeated the same movement with her other arm. "You're doing fine, Amy." He brought her hands together above her head and held both of her wrists in his left hand. "I know you're still scared," he said, his voice still low and calm. "But I made you a promise that I wouldn't hurt you and I meant it."

Tommy wrapped his shirt around her wrists before taping her hands together. "Is that too tight? Nod your head if it's hurting you or cutting off the circulation."

Amy's eyes stayed locked on his as she slowly shook her head.

"Okay, good." Tommy taped her hands to the center post on the headboard before sliding off her to stand beside the bed. He pulled the comforter off the bed and let it fall to the floor beside him. He then took the thin top sheet and tied one end around her ankle before wrapping it around the bedpost. "I'll be right back," he said as he finished tying the other leg the same way. Tommy disappeared down the hall and returned a few minutes later carrying a wild-eyed and gagged Marie. Her wrists were taped together exactly like Amy's. He sat her down in the chair next to the nightstand and taped her feet to the legs of the chair. Tommy stepped back and looked down on the wearing nothing but panties Marie. "Are you cold? Do you need a blanket or something?" He grunted when she shook her head.

Two sets of eyes watched his every move as he made his way across the room and disappeared through the master bathroom door. The sounds of rummaging and slamming drawers shut reached the two bound and gagged girls. The air from the ceiling fan cooled the beads of perspiration on the girls' skin, and Amy shivered despite the warm temperature of the room. Moments later, Tommy appeared in the doorway holding a bottle of lotion and a pair of scissors.

"It wouldn't hurt you to learn some organizational skills, little lady." He chuckled as he made his way back to the bed. He tossed the lotion onto the bed and shifted the scissors to his right hand. Amy's eyes widened with panic. She screamed even though the pillowcase over her mouth muffled the sound, and she kicked and pulled at the restraints that held her to her bed. Tommy immediately stepped back and dropped the scissors to the floor. "Shhh, it's okay now." He held his hands out in front of him. "I'm not going to hurt you, but you're going to hurt yourself if you keep fighting like that." He slowly took a step forward and leaned over Amy. "I know you're scared and I'm sorry. "He gently brushed the sweat plastered hair from her forehead with his hand. "I'm going to pick the scissors back up now and cut this tank top off, and you have got to be still while I do." He scooped the scissors off the floor. "All that jumping around might cause me to accidently cut you."

Tommy slid the scissors beneath her tank top and cut it from her body. He slid his hand beneath her back and raised her just enough to pull it from beneath her. "I'm going to tie this across your eyes and use it as a blindfold. Just stay relaxed for me." He wrapped the tank top around her head and across her eyes. He cupped her face in his hand and leaned forward, kissing her forehead. "Taking your sense of sight away causes your sense of touch to heighten, and I want you to feel everything." He raised his head slightly but continued to cup her cheek and stroke her skin with his thumb. "You really are beautiful, Amy. But I guess you already knew that, huh? You know, all I wanted to do was dance with you and maybe talk a little...So beautiful on the outside, yet so ugly on the inside."

He leaned in closer to her ear, his voice barely above a whisper. "I swore to you that I wouldn't hurt you and I won't. At first, you'll be repulsed by my touch, and the very thought of me doing the things that I am going to do to you will make you feel nauseous. But after a while, your body will start to respond and you will crave more. I promise."

Tommy stood and climbed onto the bed between her legs. He grabbed the lotion from beside her and squirted some into his hands. "I'm going to give you a little massage to help you relax." He rubbed his hands together to warm the lotion then placed both hands on her lower stomach just above her dark red panties. Her skin was a smooth contrast to his calloused hands. Slowly and softly, he slid them up her stomach toward her breasts and circled each one around the edges, his palms smearing the lotion as they made their way back down her body. "You are incredibly sexy." His voice was soft and husky as he picked up the bottle and squirted more lotion into his hands. He placed one hand on each of her thighs and with long, slow strokes, worked her muscles from the top of her knees up to her waist. After several minutes, he felt the tension start to leave her muscles as it gave way to his expert hands. Tommy glanced up at the still pursed lips and rigid jawline of his blindfolded beauty and allowed his hands to glide across her panties and back onto her stomach, kneading her muscles and caressing her skin. Up and down mixed with circular strokes, he worked every inch of her upper body and legs while avoiding her breasts and private parts until the tension left her jaw and her lips were slightly parted.

Tommy took this as the cue he had been waiting for and leaned over her body, resting his weight on his left arm beside her. The fingertips on his right hand softly caressed her right breast as he leaned in closer. His lips parted and barely made contact with the dark pink skin of her areola. His warm breath teased her nipple until it started to harden beneath his lips. He circled the hardened pebble with his tongue multiple times before gently raking his teeth across it. His lips and hot breath brought goosebumps to the surface of her skin while he worked his way up to the hollow of her neck. "I love the taste of your skin," he breathed into her flesh. He traced the outline of her jaw with his tongue to the point of her chin then worked his way back down the other side of her neck until he reached her left breast. Her nipple was already hard as he flicked it back and forth before taking it between his lips. He heard her inhale and hold her breath as he increased the suction and worked the tip with his tongue. Tommy slid his right hand down her side, onto her leg, back up her inner thigh, and stopped, the side of his palm resting on the edge of her panties. He could feel the heat starting to seep from her panty-covered mound. With soft kisses and nibbles, his lips traveled down the skin of her left side and across her belly. Tommy readjusted on the bed until he was lying between her legs. He planted his lips on the inside of her thigh and his darting tongue once again tasted her skin. Taking his time, he kissed his way to the crease of her leg then traced her skin next to her panty line. Dragging his lips across her panty-covered clit, he repeated the same onslaught of sweet torture on the other side. Tommy slipped his tongue under the edge of her panties, tracing one outer lip from top to bottom. The soft moan that escaped her lips had him grinding his hard, jean-covered cock into her bed. Her clit started to swell and was trying to poke through her panties. With light pressure, Tommy softly began to circle it with his thumb until a wet spot appeared on the red fabric covering her entrance. He stretched the panties tightly across her clit with his free hand and started a relentless attack of feather light strokes on her sensitive bundle of nerves. The muscles went tight across her abdomen and her breaths became short and fast. Tommy kept up the assault on her clit until her hips were rising to meet his hand. He stopped abruptly and held still for a few seconds. “Not yet, pretty girl. Not yet.”

Her whimper behind the gag let him know he had her exactly where he wanted her. He replaced his thumb on her clit with his tongue, the tip teasing the hard little bud back and forth then in circles. Almost immediately, her orgasm was building again. Tommy sped up until she was right on the edge and once again thrusting her hips toward him, then he stopped for a slow count to two. He repeated this process, denying her three times before he finally allowed her to explode. Tommy ripped her soaked panties to the side, slid the hood back with his tongue, and sucked her clit between his lips. Her moans were louder now and her arms and legs were flexing against her restraints. He inserted a finger inside her and just as he had planned, her g-spot was swollen and ready. He started a back and forth motion with the tip of his tongue barely touching her clit, his finger crooked and keeping time with his tongue on her g-spot. He took her to the edge until her whole body was tense then stopped, denying her once again. Her frustrated whimpers only made him harder.

He picked up where he left off, stimulating her clit and g-spot simultaneously for a five second count and then a two second pause. Not even trying to keep count on how many times he did this, Tommy continued the sweet torture for several minutes. Finally deciding to show some mercy, he inserted another finger inside her soaked pussy and increased the pressure on her g-spot. Hard and fast bumps while his tongue still worked her clit. The shirt he had used for a gag barely contained her scream as she rode the intense orgasm to the end. Tommy glanced over at Marie. Her nipples were as hard as pebbles and she was dripping from her white cotton panties into the chair she sat in. He stood, walked over to her, and removed her gag. She watched his face with wild, lust-filled eyes. Tommy slid his left hand behind her neck and gripped the hair close to her scalp, pulling back until her face was tilted toward his. He brought his fingers to her mouth. "Your friend has something for you...Taste it." Marie's mouth opened and she licked his come-soaked fingers clean, her eyes never leaving his.

Tommy turned and walked back to Amy's limp form. He removed her gag and the tape from her hands. Her eyes on his and her mouth open, she took in deep breaths. He unzipped his jeans and freed his raging hard-on. Immediately, Amy reached for his cock and tried to pull him closer. Tommy resisted her and walked to the foot of the bed, freeing her legs. “How do you want it? What’s your favorite position?” he demanded.

Without saying a word, Amy brought her knees to her chest and held them there with her hands. Tommy positioned himself between her legs and rubbed her swollen pussy with the head of his cock. “You want me to fuck you now?”

“Fuck me,” she breathed.

He circled her clit, smearing his cock with her juices. “Are you ready?” He waited for her nod. “How do you want me to fuck you?”

She moaned and reached for him, one hand grabbing his ass and pulling him closer. “Just fuck me, damn it. Fuck me now.”

Tommy slipped the head inside her and allowed her to pull him tighter. “If you want me to stop, I will. All you have to do is say so.”

“Will you just do it already?” she pleaded. “I want you to fuck me. Fuck me hard...Please...Just fuck me. Make me come again."

Chapter 4

Tommy slung his sweat towel over his shoulder and exited his truck. Shinedown was already ripping through his Bluetooth headset and the beta-alanine in his pre-workout was burning though his veins like hot lava. His fast walk was closer to a jog as he headed for the gym door and swiped his key card. The anticipation of the pain he was about to inflict on his body, the feeling of the pump as his skin stretched tight across his muscles, and the exhaustion he would feel in an hour when he exited these doors knowing he had left it all on the floor, was exhilarating. After catching his whore wife cheating, he had turned to working out as a form of therapy. No matter how bad things got, he could always count on the weights to take all of his emotional pain and transfer it to a physical pain. In addition to the wonderful things it did for him mentally, it was also starting to have a positive effect on his body. Not even close to where he wanted to be, but getting there.

Tommy looked around the gym and noticed he was all alone except for one woman. One of the reasons he loved working out at Anytime Fitness was he could come late at night after most people had gone home and not have to wait on equipment. One last look at the woman in white yoga pants and a black long-sleeved shirt, and Tommy headed for the bench press. He loaded a forty-five-pound plate on each side of the bar, swung his arms back and forth a few times to stretch, and laid down to blast through a couple of warm up sets. Eight minutes later, his muscles were warm, his shoulders were loose, and he was ready to push some weight.

He gripped the bar just slightly more than shoulder width apart and took a couple of deep breaths. Tommy glanced at the additional plates he had added. He knew he was pushing his luck, but he needed it to hurt in a big way tonight.

He opened and closed his grip a few times and checked the space between his hands again. "Fuck that whore bitch," he mumbled. His pecs came alive as he pushed the weighted bar from its rack. His heartbeat quickened as it pumped blood to the tearing muscles and every inch of his body went rigid. Every nerve, every piece of tissue, and every muscle became a conduit for all the rage and all the disappointment he felt. In one massive channel, hate and bitterness flowed all the way to his chest where it manifested itself as strength and allowed him to lift heavier and push harder than ever before.

Tommy once again stared at the bar above him as he tightened his grip for his fourth and final set of bench presses. His pecs were screaming for mercy and he honestly doubted whether or not he had another set of ten left in him.

C'mon, Tommy. Reach deep, man. One more set.

He sucked in a deep breath and let it out slowly.

"I deserve a man with a nice body." Nicole's voice echoed in his ears as he heaved the bar up and brought it down to his chest.

One...

"A man who dresses better than you."

Two...

"A man with enough money to give me the things I deserve."

Three...

"A man I can be proud of."

Four...

A single tear slid down his cheek and joined the puddle of sweat on the bench around his head.

Five...

He furiously blinked his eyes to clear his vision and fight the weakness the tears represented.

Six...

"He's all of those things."

Seven...

"He's the man you'll never be."

Eight...

Tommy groaned under the weight and held his arms locked for a second. *Two more, you pussy. Two mother fuckin more.*

Nine...

"Baby, wait up. I'm coming with you. Fuck this loser."

Ten...

Tommy wiped the sweat from his face and then the bench before heading for a drink of water. He rounded the corner leading out to the main lobby where the water fountain was located. The view that greeted him made him forget all about his cheating ex-wife. The white yoga pants were stretched tightly across her beautiful ass as she bent over drinking from the fountain. The sweat from her workout made the thin material see through and was doing a fine job of showing off the skimpy red thong she was wearing beneath them. Her tanned skin was a perfect contrast bleeding through the wet material of her pants. Tommy felt the stirring in his loose-fitting shorts and failed miserably at trying to pry his eyes off her derriere.

"See something you like?" Her voice managed to do what he hadn't been able to.

Tommy looked up at the smiling woman and saw that she was looking over her shoulder at him. "Ahem." Tommy cleared his throat and ran his hand though his sweat soaked hair. "I uh..." His red cheeks spread into an embarrassed smile. "I guess it's probably a little late for *Hi, how are you,* huh?"

She straightened up from the water fountain and turned to face him. "I guess it depends on exactly what you were doing to me in that dirty mind of yours." She winked and stuck out her hand. "I'm Elizabeth. My friends call me Liz."

Tommy couldn't help but notice how soft her hand was as he gently gripped it in his. "I'm Tommy. Are we friends or should I call you Elizabeth?"

Liz held on to his hand and stepped forward until her breasts were touching his chest. Her voice had a hint of a Spanish accent to it that only made her sexier. "Again, I guess it depends on what you were just doing to me while I was bent over that fountain." She eased forward, grinding her waist into his crotch. "It certainly feels like we've reached the friend stage."

Before he could reply, Liz turned, walked down the hall, and disappeared through the lady's restroom door.

Tommy adjusted himself and cursed his gym shorts then headed over to the pec deck to do some flies.

Seven, eight, nine. Tommy kept his eyes closed and focused on squeezing out each rep. He thoroughly enjoyed the pump as he forced more blood into his chest muscles. "Ten," he mumbled to no one in particular and allowed the arms of the machine to return to their resting position in a slow, controlled negative. Tommy opened his eyes and had to blink a couple of times to be sure he was seeing what stood before him. Liz was standing directly across from him at the squat rack with her back to him. She had lost the black, long sleeved T-shirt and was now in just her white sports bra. He allowed his eyes another look at her magnificent rear end. The damp cotton that had so generously revealed her red panties now revealed the lack thereof. His pulsed quickened and all the blood that he had been pumping into his chest made a beeline straight for his pants.

Damn, he thought. *It's not even my birthday and this little honey clearly wants me as bad as I want her.*

Tommy gripped the handles on the pec deck once more and started his next set, while his mind worked out the details on exactly how to proceed. This time with his eyes open and glued to hers in a wall-length mirror.

Liz stepped under the weightless squat bar and lifted it into the air. With her eyes locked on his in the mirror, she squatted ever so slowly and just a little too seductively to be considered good or proper form. Tommy watched her sexy body dipping down until she was in the sitting position and imagined her sliding down on his hard cock the same way. He stood and headed over to the dumbbell rack and chose two sixty pounders for his flat bench dumbbell presses. He placed the dumbbells on the floor beside the middle bench in the row of utility benches and took a seat. Tommy stared into the mirror behind the rack and watched Liz make her way to the bench beside him to his left.

"Mind some company?" Her voice seemed just a tad bit sultrier than it had during their introductions.

"Would welcome it." Tommy smiled. "But from the look of things, I thought you were working glutes, not chest."

"Oh, I am." She smiled a little too sweetly and pushed her chosen bench a little farther away from him. "I'm about to do my favorite exercise."

"Oh yeah? And what might that be?" Tommy dipped his shoulders and gripped the dumbbells on the floor beside him, bringing them to rest on his knees.

Liz stepped around to the side of her bench and leaned backward until just her shoulders and upper back rested on the bench. Her feet were wider than shoulder width apart and flat on the floor less than a foot from where Tommy sat. Her body was suspended in midair and her wet, see-through white yoga pants cupped her pussy perfectly, leaving nothing for his imagination.

"Oh shit. Hip thrusts," Tommy groaned.

Liz dipped her ass toward the floor and thrust her hips back up and held them there for a two second count.

Tommy's hard-on raged beneath his shorts as he imagined dropping to his knees right in front of her and tasting her sweet pussy.

"Enjoying the show?" Her voice brought him out of his lustful imaginings as she finished her set and took a seat on the edge of her bench.

His eyes met hers above her cocky little smile, but he remained silent.

"Well, Stud, I certainly hope you are." She ran her hands down the top of her legs and back up her inner thighs. "I'd hate to be working out this hard for nothing."

He brought his knees together and balanced the two dumbbells with his left hand and her eyes followed his right hand as he adjusted his unruly cock. "I believe it's having the desired effect." His lust-filled voice was low and tight.

"Good," was her only response as she slid back into position for another set.

Tommy watched her for four more reps then tore his eyes away from her and laid back to start his own set. He pushed the dumbbells toward the ceiling then lowered them to his sides, doing his best to feel the burn. But the only burn he could think about was that hot, wet pussy beside him.

He let the weights fall to the floor on each side of him and stared in amazement as Liz swung her leg over him and straddled his upper thighs.

"I'm all done with my workout now, but I wanted to tell you it was nice meeting you." She leaned forward and ran her hands across his chest and down his body to his stomach.

"Uh, yeah. It's been a pleasure meeting you as well," Tommy stammered.

"I'm in serious need of a shower." She continued her downward path and slid her hands over the bulge in his shorts. "Looks like you could use one too." She gently squeezed his cock and stood up then disappeared toward the showers.

***

Tommy pushed open the shower room door marked Ladies and looked around. The steam drifting over the top of the stall door at the very end on the right announced its occupant. His heart seemed to speed up with each footstep as he made his way toward the sexy little flirt who had been tormenting him. His cock throbbed with excitement as his mind played out all the scenarios her teasing had promised. Tommy kicked off his tennis shoes then quickly undressed, tossing his clothes over the bench next to her gym bag. His hand involuntarily reached down and grabbed the throbbing member between his legs and squeezed as he gently pulled the shower door open and stepped inside.

Liz had both hands planted on the wall in front of her and her face pointed up toward the shower nozzle. The hot water running down her long brown hair and over her thick ass had him fighting for control. Tommy's cock pulsed in his hand as he stroked it. He watched little rivers of water flow from her fleshy cheeks and down the backs of her meaty thighs. Unable to only watch this beauty any longer, Tommy stepped forward and placed his left hand next to hers on the wall. His right hand slid between her legs as his lips touched her ear.

"You need some help washing or should we skip right to the good stuff?"

Liz screamed and spun around to face him. "What the fuck are you doing?" She planted her back against the wall she had been leaning against only seconds before and covered her breasts with her hands.

Tommy took a step back from the enraged woman and tilted his head to the side to avoid the spraying water hitting him in the face. "I decided to take you up on your invitation."

"My what?" she hissed. "What in the hell would make you think I was inviting you to shower with me?"

Tommy stared at her for several long seconds before replying. "You said 'I'm in serious need of a shower? It looks like you could use one too?' That, after you'd been teasing me and touching me all night?"

Liz burst out laughing and let her eyes wander down his body to his shrinking cock. "You can't be serious. Do you really think I would want to have sex with you?"

The red creeped up his neck until it reached his cheeks. "Well yeah, I mean...that's what I thought you wanted." Tommy reached up and rubbed the back of his neck. "You have to admit, you were coming on to me pretty hard tonight."

"Coming on to you?" she sneered. "You think I actually want you?" Liz removed her hands from her breasts and held them out to her side. "Look at me. Do you know how hard I've had to work to build this?"

Tommy cleared his throat. "Well yeah, I can see that and trust me, it's paid off. You look amazing." He flashed his biggest smile. "Hey, look. No harm no foul, right? I guess it's just a misunderstanding. I'm sorry I misread what was going on."

"You are damned right it's paid off." Liz pointed at his naked body and shook her head. "And there's no way in hell I'd let *that* anywhere near something like this." She pointed at herself. "It's just fun getting guys like you all riled up and seeing you want what you can't have." Her voice was hard as she flung her hand toward the stall door. "Now get the hell out of here and throw my towel over the door on your way out."

The muscle in Tommy's jaw ticked as he slowly nodded his head before he turned and exited the shower, leaving the door open. He made it halfway down the narrow hall between the shower stalls before he stopped dead in his tracks. His chest expanded as the air filled his lungs in a slow and controlled deep breath. Tommy unhurriedly turned and made his way back down the hall. His jaw clenched with each step. His shoulder dipped and he scooped the white towel from the bench next to her gym bag and threw it against the back wall of the shower. Liz's eyes darted from the towel soaking up water on the shower floor then back to Tommy.

Tommy's eyes were locked on hers. "You should have asked me nicely, little girl."

"Wha...what?" Liz's eyes widened at the intensity in his voice and she stepped back. Her back was against the wall for the second time tonight.

"That's the problem with women like you, always judging a book by its cover." His husky voice was low and controlled.

"Look, Tony—"

"—It's Tommy, not Tony," he growled and stepped in close to her.

Immediately, she placed both palms on his chest and attempted to push him back. "Tony, Tommy. You're all the same to me. A piece of advice for you before you get the hell out of here. Dress up the cover and maybe someone will want to read the book."

Tommy grabbed her wrists and brought both of her hands to the wall above her head before placing his forehead against hers. "Sweetheart, when I get done with you, you're going to want your very own copy."

"You arrogant ass..."

Tommy silenced her verbal assault by crushing his lips to hers. He gripped both her wrists with his left hand and nudged her left foot to the side with his own bare foot. He slid his right hand between her legs, split his fingers, and started a slow, rhythmic massage on her pussy lips. His head still held hers against the wall.

"Stop that, you fucking pig," she said into his mouth.

Tommy leaned back until his mouth was only inches away from hers. "Oh, I'll stop. But when I do, you'll beg me to start again."

The water from the shower served as a lubricant for his two middle fingers as he slid them between her lips. Pinching her clit between his thumb and forefinger, he felt her body vibrate as she moaned. Tommy repeated the same massage technique as before, rocking his fingers into her opening while never letting her clit slip from his grasp.

"You can't do this. You have to stop," she moaned.

"Feels good don't it, Elizabeth? I guess I'll call you Elizabeth since I'm not good enough to be your friend." Tommy chuckled. "You're about to forget all about the less than perfect cover." He leaned down and took her nipple between his teeth, softly raking them across it until it slid from his mouth. Quickly sucking it back between his lips, he ran his tongue around it. Her moan was barely louder than the noise of the running water, but loud enough to serve as the encouragement he'd been waiting for. Tommy changed his technique by placing the top of his middle finger over her swelling clit and gently probing the edge of her entrance with the pad of his finger. He brought his lips back to hers and, this time, her lips parted and her tongue darted out to meet him, but Tommy moved his head as her tongue touched his lips. He nudged her wet hair away from her ear with his nose and lightly ran his tongue behind it. He felt her hips pushing forward, trying to increase the pressure from his hand. In one swift yet fluid movement, Tommy removed his hand from between her thighs, gripped her ass, and spun her around until she was facing the wall. He still held her wrists above her head with his left hand. He pressed his hips into her ass until his hard cock was nestled between her cheeks, and then slipped his right hand around her and back onto her pussy. There was no mistaking her slick, wet arousal for the water from the shower. Tommy slid his middle finger inside her and brought his thumb to rest on the rigid nub pultruding from beneath its hood. He kissed her right shoulder blade and worked his way across her back and up to her neck. The relentless attack of the come here motion he was performing on her g-spot mixed with the pad of his thumb sliding across her clit had Liz's head hanging down and her knees bending. The cries of ecstasy told Tommy her orgasm was approaching at a rapid rate. Wanting to prove a point, Tommy increased both the pressure on her g-spot and the speed on her clit.

Tommy released her wrists and she leaned forward the last few inches, resting her head on the wall. She brought her hands up, cupping her breasts, and started rolling her nipples between her thumb and forefingers. "Oh fuck, Tommy. I'm coming," she moaned." Liz's thighs tightened around his hand until she finished riding the intense orgasm to the end.

When she finished, Tommy removed his hand from her body, turned, and walked back out of the shower.

"Wait! That's it?" she yelled and rushed out behind him.

Tommy spun around and slipped his hands beneath her armpits. He lifted her until her legs wrapped around his waist, turned, and stepped forward, placing her back against the closed door of an empty shower stall. He reached between them and gripped his dick in his hand.

"Yes. Fuck me," she growled. "Give me that cock. Let me feel it inside me right now."

Tommy slid the head of his cock down the center of her wet pussy until he felt the heat of her opening. Without warning, he slammed his full length inside of her until his balls were tight against her ass. He slid his hands beneath her ass and cupped her cheeks. There was nothing gentle about the way he bounced her up and down on his cock. Her moans echoed in rhythm with each powerful thrust.

Liz leaned forward off the glass and wrapped her arms around his neck. She gripped his hair with both hands and kissed him hard. "Fuck, Tommy. I'm going to come."

Tommy eased one hand over until his middle finger was rubbing his cock as it slid in and out of her pussy. He smeared the juices on her ass and placed the tip of his finger at her entrance. Each time she came down on his cock, his finger slid into her ass. The stimulation of both holes sent her over the edge.

"Oh shit!" she yelled. "I'm coming. Fuck me...I'm coming."

Tommy let her ride out the orgasm then carried her over to the bench where her gym bag was lying. He straddled the bench and laid her on her back, folding her legs up until her knees were touching her chest.

He dropped his hips just enough so that each stroke would drive his cock upward into her g-spot. Thankful that his pre-workout hadn't completely worn off yet, he picked up the same exhausting pace he had just brought her to orgasm with. The constant pressure on her g-spot had her building again in a matter of moments.

"Yes, just like that." She reached forward and grabbed his hips, pulling him into her. "Fuck me...Fuck me harder."

Tommy pulled on her legs until they were flat against his chest and wrapped his arms around them for leverage. He drove his cock into her as hard and as fast as he could until she let out a scream and squirted her orgasm, soaking them both.

"Holy fuck," she gasped and let her hands fall to her sides.

He spread her legs and slipped his hand between them, starting a fast-paced slide over her clit.

"Oh shit, Tommy," she groaned. "I need a break.

He kept up the stimulation on her clit and continued to fuck her, driving his hips upward.

"Tommy...Oh fuck...Tommy." Her eyes went wide and she threw back her head, her body bowing up off the bench. "I'm coming...motherfucker, I'm coming again."

Tommy fucked her for several more strokes before pulling his cock out and shooting six long spurts of come all over her belly and pussy. When he had sufficiently recovered, he grabbed his clothes, gave her a smile and a wink, then turned and walked away.

Chapter 5

"Son of a bitch," Tommy mumbled and tossed the chipped piece of tile to the side. He was trying his best to finish setting all the tile today so he could collect his check then move on to the next job. Not that he really wanted to leave this job. The scenery was pretty spectacular and though he wasn't quite sure, it almost seemed like his customer was a little flirty at times.

"Is something wrong?" she asked from the doorway.

"Shit!" Tommy dropped his tape measure and whipped his head around to face her. Amanda Riggs was drop dead gorgeous and she knew it. Tommy tore his eyes away from those long, sexy legs, which were flowing out of her denim shorts that had been cut off just below her ass. Being on his knees and the scenarios that were running through his head only made the moment all that more awkward. "Sorry, I was kind of engrossed in what I was doing and didn't hear you walk up behind me."

"I didn't mean to startle you. I thought I heard you talking and came to see if you were calling for me."

"Oh. No, ma'am." He willed his eyes to stay locked on her face and ignore what the skin-tight T-shirt and lack of a bra was failing to hide. "One of the tiles chipped while I was installing it and now I have to re-cut one to replace it...I guess you could say I was letting it know how much I didn't appreciate it." Tommy chuckled at his corny joke and secretly cussed himself for acting like a kid going through puberty.

Amanda took a step closer to Tommy, which brought her denim-covered crotch only a couple of inches away from his face. "Well, since I'm here. Is there anything I can do for you?"

Shit, Tommy, think man. Is she hitting on you or offering a glass of water?

He reached up and grabbed the vanity top to pull himself to his feet. Was it his imagination, or could he actually smell her arousal?

Tommy cleared his throat as he turned to face her. "I...no. I think I have everything I need. But, thank you."

"Okay." Amanda reached up and brushed a piece of tile mortar from his cheek. "Let me know if that changes...I'll be around."

His eyes were glued to her legs and ass as she disappeared back through the master bathroom door.

Tommy finished marking the tile that needed to be cut and made his way through the house and out the pool bath door to where his tile saw was set up in the backyard next to the pool deck. He lined the mark up with the blade and flipped the switch. The tile saw roared to life and sliced through the piece of ceramic like it was hot butter. He killed the power and inspected his work. Tommy Reid considered himself somewhat of an artist. He took a lot of pride in his work, and knowing that every job he left was perfect gave him an extreme feeling of accomplishment. Almost anyone could set tile, but he could create masterpieces and he knew it.

"Damn, Tommy boy, it's a sin to be this good," he muttered and turned to head back inside to install the work of art.

Her white bikini bottoms left little to the imagination and yet had his imagination working overtime. The way she sat, straddling the chaise lounge chair with her legs wide open as she rubbed suntan oil on her midsection and bare tits, made him very thankful for the long shirt he'd chosen to wear today. Tommy's professionalism kicked in and he recovered fast. He kept his eyes straight ahead as he continued toward the door.

"Hey, Tommy?" she called.

Oh shit. Just keep walking and pretend you didn't hear her. Don't mix business with pleasure, man.

Tommy twisted the doorknob and disappeared inside. He no sooner made it back to the master bath than he heard the back door close, announcing that someone had come inside.

Damn it. Damn it. Damn it.

Tommy adjusted his hard-on and pulled his shirt back down over it just as she rounded the corner holding a bottle of tanning lotion. Her bare tits were well worth every penny she had spent on them, and her nipples were so hard they appeared to be brittle.

She smiled sweetly when Tommy's eyes finally made their way to hers. "I was calling for you but I guess you didn't hear me."

"You were?" He tried to act normal and not let her see the affect her half-piece bathing suit was having on him. "I'm sorry. I kind of get caught up in my work sometimes and tune out everything around me."

"I was hoping you could help me out and rub some lotion on my back." She pushed the bottle of tanning lotion toward him.

As if he had no control whatsoever, Tommy's hand reached out to take the bottle. "Are you sure? I mean...you want me to..." He glanced down at her store-bought beauties and then forced his eyes back to her face. "Are you sure?"

"Yes, Tommy. I'm sure." She laughed and turned around, pulling her hair to the side as she did. "I can never get it rubbed in evenly and it messes up my tan."

He let out the breath he hadn't realized he was holding and squeezed some lotion into his hand before placing the bottle on the vanity top. Her skin was smooth to his touch and he hoped the lotion helped mask the roughness of his calloused hands.

Oh, she's definitely hitting on me. Even a fool like me can read these signs.

Tommy let his hands glide down her toned back to the top of her bikini bottoms, where he traced the elastic band with his thumb before sliding back up her to her shoulders then down the middle of her back again.

She let out a soft moan then turned to face him. Tommy let her twist in his hands until he had her hips in his grip.

"Thank you so much." She rose up on her toes and kissed his cheek. "I'll be out back sunning if you need me."

He watched her walk back through the door for the second time in the past hour, leaving him confused about what he thought he was reading, also for the second time in an hour.

***

Tommy stepped back to admire his finished project then snapped a few pics with his cell phone to be printed off later for the photo album. He had finished cleaning up and the only thing left to do was to load that beast of a tile saw. He took one last appreciative look at his work and flipped the switch, killing the light. He exited the bathroom and headed back down the hallway that lead to the pool bath and back yard. Tommy slid open the pocket door just about the same time the shower door announced its disapproval of being slid open on its track. The overhead light danced across her wet skin, making her appear to be glowing. The urge to taste every drop of water that clung to her sun kissed body overpowered any professionalism he would have normally felt. His eyes followed her hand as it slid across her stomach and down the top of her thigh, raking the beads of water onto the shower floor. Her hairless pussy appeared to be freshly waxed. Tommy's cock strained against his jeans as the realization hit him. She really had been coming on to him this whole time and he had been a fool to doubt the signs.

"Tommy, could you be a doll and hand me a towel, please?"

Tommy ignored her request as his eyes locked on hers. He stepped forward and hooked his arm around her waist, drawing her wet body to him. His mouth met hers as he gripped the back of her head with his free hand. He lowered his hand from her waist and gripped her ass tightly, pulling her crotch into his throbbing cock.

Amanda slid both hands between them to his chest and pushed him backward. "Tommy! What are you doing?"

He grabbed the hem of his shirt and pulled it over his head. "Let's cut the games, Mandy. We both know that we both want this." Tommy tossed his shirt to the side and closed the distance her shove had created between them.

"Have you lost your mind?" She pushed him again. "I ask you for a towel and you take that to mean I want you?"

The lines in Tommy's forehead deepened and he took another step back until his ass came to rest on the vanity top. "Are you telling me that you haven't been flirting with me the whole time I've been remodeling your master shower?" The blood left his pants and started to creep up his neck? "Or that you haven't been openly coming on to me all day today?"

"Oh, my God. That's the problem with you guys who don't have meaningful careers or higher educations." Amanda's voice had climbed a few octaves and was starting to sound more like a squeal. "You see a beautiful woman and, if she's nice to you, you automatically start thinking she wants you."

"What?" Tommy pushed off the granite top. "Are you fucking serious right now?"

"Just get the hell out of my house before I call the cops and have you removed."

"You are one crazy bitch, you know that?" He flexed and unflexed his fists. "You need to put some damned clothes on and cut me a check. Then I'll leave."

"Get out now, you low life pervert. I'll mail the damned check," she almost screeched.

Tommy scooped up his shirt and stormed out the back door. He tossed the shirt on top of his saw then pushed it around the house to where his truck was backed into her driveway.

She's fucking insane. There's no way I read all of that wrong…no way. She's been teasing me all day.

He slammed the tailgate shut then climbed into the cab and fired the engine up. The truck tires squealed, leaving black tread marks on the immaculate driveway as he pulled into the street.

Chapter 6

Tommy closed the front door behind him and kicked his work boots off. Pulling his shirt over his head, he made his way down the hallway and into his bedroom. He tossed his keys toward the dresser and cursed under his breath as they slid across the smooth top and landed on the floor beside his bed. He ignored the keys and stepped into the master bath. Tommy finished removing his clothes and stepped into the shower to wash away a long days' worth of work and frustration. The hot water soaked into his tense muscles and calmed him.

What the hell is wrong with women these days? Tease a man to the point of breaking and then shoot him down.

Tommy grabbed the bar of soap and stepped away from the comfort of the soothing water to lather up. He washed the sweat from the day's labor away and stepped back into the streams of comfort that awaited him.

I should have shown her...

Tommy killed the water and snatched the towel from where it hung over the shower door.

I should have taken her right there in the shower. There's no way she wasn't trying to instigate something acting the way she was...

He toweled his body dry. Images of Amanda in her various stages of undress and then complete nudity had his cock coming to life.

I was professional; she's the one that kept teasing me with her sexy body and open-ended comments...

He hung the towel back over the shower door and hit the light switch as he stepped through the doorway into his room.

"What the fuck?" Tommy stopped just inside his room and stared.

Her blonde hair hung down over her bare shoulders and flowed onto the pillow she had stuffed behind her back. She was completely nude and sitting on his bed with her back against the headboard. Her knees were up and her right hand was between her legs, rubbing her pussy. And from the sound of things, it was a very wet pussy.

"Who the hell are you?" Tommy glanced around the room to see if he had any more unannounced visitors before turning his attention back to the pretty stranger in his bed.

She held his gaze, but her only response to his question was to bring her fingers to her mouth and lick them clean before returning them to her pussy.

The irony of being shot down and then having a naked woman in his bed—who was clearly enjoying herself—all within a few hours, wasn't lost on Tommy. But if there was one thing he had learned the hard way, it was not to trust everything you see when it comes to women hitting on you.

Tommy watched her fingers dip inside her pussy and then circle her clit a few times before trying again.

"Hey, uh..." He chuckled. "Look, I'm not saying I'm not enjoying the show or anything, but I'd kind of like to know the name of the main character, if that's okay with you."

"Would you like to help me?" She slid her fingers down the inside of her lips and spread them apart.

Her voice tugged at a memory but he couldn't quite place it. "What I'd like to do is know who the fuck you are and how you got in here," he demanded, his voice taking on a hard edge. "Did Amanda send you over here?"

"Oh, Thomas, you don't remember me?"

Thomas? Nobody called him Thomas, not even his parents.

"Okay, enough of this shit. You need to get the fuck out of here." Tommy stepped closer to the bed and grabbed her arm. "And you can tell that bitch, Amanda, she can kiss my ass."

"Wait, stop. It's me, Marie. And I don't know any Amanda."

"Yeah well, I don't know a Marie, so you have to go." He pulled on her arm to encourage her along.

"From the club? You had the hots for my friend Amy. You broke into her house and tied us both up...Remember now?"

Tommy let go of her arm and stepped back. "I uh..." He quickly glanced toward his bedroom door again then back to her. "How did you get in here? And why? Why are you here?"

Marie giggled and slid her legs over the side of his bed. "Boy, you look like you just saw a ghost. You can stop checking the door. I'm alone."

His eyes darted back to the door in spite of her claims then locked on her again. "I want some fucking answers. How'd you get in?"

"Well, I was going to ring the doorbell but when I checked, the door was unlocked, so I came on in. I called your name but you didn't answer, and then I heard the shower and thought a little surprise would help me get what I came for."

He stared at her in silence for what seemed like several minutes but couldn't have been more than a few seconds. "What did you come for?"

Marie pushed herself off the bed and slowly took a step toward him. "I can't stop thinking about it. When I close my eyes, I can still see you and what you were doing to

Amy." She stopped just a few inches from him and placed her hands on his chest. "I want that. I want you to make me feel the way you made her feel."

Tommy searched her face for some sort of clue that this was some kind of trick or game.

"Please, Thomas?" She slid her right hand down and started stroking his cock back to life.

"Tommy. Nobody calls me Thomas." He tried to ignore the sensations of her soft hand stroking and massaging his dick. "How did you find me?"

Marie leaned forward and took his nipple between her lips and sucked hard before looking back up at him. "My cousin is the bartender at the One Night Stand. He got your name from your credit card receipt." She flicked his nipple with her tongue. "Your address is a matter of public records." She moved to the opposite side of his chest and clamped her lips around his other nipple, sucking hard while flicking the tip of her tongue across the tight nub.

A moan escaped his lips and he brought his hand to the back of her head and gripped her hair. He pulled her mouth off his chest.

Her hand tightened around his cock. "I can feel how bad you want me...just take me. I want it too."

The muscle along his jaw twitched as he stared down at her. "Little girl." His voice took on a hard and husky edge. "This is your one and only chance to stop this and leave. If you don't...I'm going to wreak havoc on that pretty body of yours, and I swear on my life that every single fuckin inch of you will feel me when I'm done."

Marie cupped his balls with her left hand and gently squeezed his cock with her right.

Tommy released her hair and dropped his hand to her waist. He spun her around and backed her against the wall. Then he slid his right hand between her legs and cupped her pussy, with his eyes once again locked on hers. "I'm about to own this," he growled.

She crushed her lips to his, her tongue probing his lips.

Tommy reached out and wrapped his left hand in her hair close to the back of her neck. He tilted her head back and to the side, exposing her throat. He kissed the center of her throat then the side of her neck and slid his tongue up to her ear. "From this point on, you don't do anything that I don't give you permission to do." His voice was low and intense. "You don't touch me unless I tell you to." He nipped the bottom of her ear with his teeth. "You don't come unless I tell you to." He turned her head until she was facing him. "Are we clear?"

A slight nod was her only response and Tommy felt her pussy clench in his palm. "Good," he replied and slipped two fingers inside her. "I am now in control of your pleasure." He teased her lips with the tip of his tongue. "If you obey me, I will continue to pleasure you." He let go of her hair, giving her control of her head. "If you challenge me, I will torture you and never give you the release your body craves."

Marie moaned and squeezed her muscles around his fingers while staring at him with questioning eyes.

"Yes, that's okay," he whispered and brought his lips to hers. He tapped the defined ridges of her g-spot with the pads of his fingers while their mouths hungrily devoured one another. Tommy removed his fingers and smeared her juices on her clit before sliding them back inside her. He lowered his head and gently raked his teeth across her nipple then sucked it between his lips. Without warning, he started fucking her pussy hard and fast with his fingers while sliding his thumb across her clit with every stroke.

Marie held her breath and her eyes widened as the intensity of his relentless attack on her clit and g-spot brought her pussy to life and her orgasm started to build.

Tommy released her nipple from his mouth and looked up at her. "Communication is the key here. You tell me when you're close, when you're about to come. If you come without telling me beforehand, I'll stop and make you leave. Understand?" Without waiting for a reply, he took her nipple back between his lips and circled it with his tongue. He curled his fingers, raking them hard across her g-spot each time he pulled out, while his thumb still slide across her clit.

Her stomach tightened and she grabbed the back of his head, pulling him tighter to her breast before remembering her orders and quickly snatching her hands away. "I'm close," she moaned.

Tommy sped up his attack on her pussy.

"Oh, fuck," she panted. "I'm going to come."

He immediately slowed down, prolonging her orgasm but keeping her right on the edge.

"No," she whined. "Don't do that."

He sped back up for a couple of strokes then slowed back down to a steady, monotonous rhythm.

"Oh, Tommy?" she moaned again.

He moved his lips up to her ear and his voice was barely above a whisper. "What do you want, little girl?"

"You know what I want. Please?" she begged.

Tommy fell into a rhythm of four quick strokes and four slow strokes. "Tell me," he demanded.

"I want to come," she groaned.

He suddenly stopped the stimulation. "I can't hear you. What did you say?"

"Fuck, Tommy," she shouted. "You got me right there. Please don't stop." Her pussy clamped down on his fingers over and over as she tried to keep the orgasm building. "Please, let me come."

He slowly started the finger fucking and clit massage again. "You want to come for me? Is that what you're telling me?"

"God yes," she whimpered. "Can I kiss you?"

Tommy nodded and increased the speed of his fingers.

She slipped both hands behind his head and pulled his mouth to hers. Then she begged again, "Please, Tommy. Make me come."

He sped up a little more and increased the pressure on her g-spot. "Are you going to come hard for me if I let you orgasm, little girl?"

"Yes," she moaned and leaned her head back onto the wall.

"Okay." Tommy smiled. "Since you asked me so nicely, you can come."

He slid his left hand down to her ass and pulled her tight until her leg was pinned against his. He left his fingers inside her and fingered her hard with a come here motion while rubbing her clit back and forth with his thumb.

"Holy fuck," she groaned.

"That's it, pretty girl. Come for me."

"Oh, God. Don't stop, Tommy. I'm going to come." She leaned forward off the wall and pressed her head to his.

"Yes, ride it out," Tommy whispered. "Come hard for me."

"Fuuuuck!" she screamed. "I'm coming." Her pussy tightened around his fingers and her whole body went rigid as she exploded into his hand.

Marie slid her hands down to his shoulders and jumped into his arms, wrapping her legs around his waist. "Fuck me." She reached behind her and grabbed his cock, guiding it to her pussy. "I need you inside me right now."

Tommy spun around and laid her back on the bed. "I'll decide when you need me inside you." He pried her legs from around his waist and used them as leverage to turn her around until her head was hanging off the edge of the bed. "First, I want to feel that sexy mouth on me." He gripped his cock and rubbed the head across her lips.

Marie's tongue darted out and licked the pre-come that was leaking from his slit before sliding her lips over the crown.

Tommy eased his hips forward and groaned as the warmth of her mouth enveloped his throbbing cock. He grabbed both of her breasts and rolled the nipples between his thumb and forefinger while he slowly fucked her mouth. The sight of his cock disappearing past her lips, mixed with the sensation of her tongue sliding along the underside of his length, had him quickly approaching the point of no return. He leaned forward and braced himself on his left elbow on the bed then reached his right hand under her ass and buried his fingers in her pussy again. Her moans around his cock had him fighting for control. He used his lips to slide the hood back, exposing her clit, before taking it gently between his lips. He alternated between gently raking his teeth across her clit and circling it with his tongue, sliding his fingers inside her each time his teeth brushed across her and back out each time his tongue circled her tight little berry.

She pulled her mouth off his cock, wrapped her hand around him, and let out a long, painful moan. “Damn it. You’re going to make me come again.” She raised her hips, driving her pussy tighter to his face. He sucked her clit up tighter between his lips and flicked it side to side with his tongue as fast as he could without stopping the steady fucking with his fingers. Her moans were continuous and her breathing was fast.

“Fuck, Tommy. I’m coming again,” she yelled and shot her hips straight up with so much force, it pushed Tommy’s face off her. Tommy lowered his weight on her and pushed her hips back to the bed. He took her clit back between his lips and continued the onslaught of pleasure without giving her a break. He backed off on the pressure on her sensitive nub but still worked it with the tip of his tongue in short, fast strokes.

Her nails dug into the sheet. “Fuck, fuck, fuck, fuck, fuck,” she chanted

Tommy sucked a little harder and flattened out his tongue across her clit.

"I'm gonna come…I'm gonna come," she gasped. Her tiny fists balled the sheet up in her hands and she arched her hips up until only her shoulders and feet were planted on the bed.

He leaned back and slid his fingers out of her then started gently slapping her clit, over and over again, as fast as he could with his open hand.

"Shiiiiiit!" she screamed and then went silent as her come sprayed her thighs and the bed between her legs. She let out the breath she had been holding and let her hips settle back onto the bed. "I'm so sorry," she whined and searched his face for signs of anger or disappointment. "I've never peed during sex before. I'm sorry, I…"

The look of confusion and embarrassment on her face made Tommy feel a little bad for her. "Oh, little girl, you didn't pee. You squirted. Now flip over and turn around," he demanded. "I'm not waiting any longer for that sweet pussy of yours."

Tommy straightened up and helped her flip over onto her stomach. "Turn around," he demanded again and then helped her up to her hands and knees when she complied.

He positioned the head of his cock at her entrance with his hand and slid it from her opening down to her clit then back up again.

"Fuck me, Tommy." She reached between her legs, trying to grab his cock. "I can't wait to feel you inside me."

He slowly pushed all the way inside her until his hips were tight against her ass. "Fuck," he moaned. "Your pussy feels so good wrapped around me."

"Come on, damn it. I need for you to fuck me hard."

Tommy gripped both of her hips and slowly pulled his length from her then slammed it back in and held it there.

"Oh, shit. Yes, like that."

He placed one foot on the bed beside her, allowing him to control the angle and keep the head of his cock hitting her g-spot. Still gripping her hips, he slid one hand over until his thumb could play with her ass. He picked up his rhythm until his breathing was short and labored. "Fuck me, baby. You gotta come for me. I can't hold back much longer."

He slammed his cock into her over and over until he felt her body go tense again.

"I'm going to come, Tommy. Fuck me, I'm going to come again."

Tommy brought his thumb to his mouth and wet it with his saliva. "That's it, sexy, come for me." He smeared his saliva on her tight little asshole then eased his thumb inside her.

"Motherfucker, I'm coming," she screamed as her pussy convulsed around his cock, milking the come from his balls.

Chapter 7

Liz paced back and forth across her living room before sitting down for the third time in three minutes. She stared at the blank TV while subconsciously smoothing her short little sundress across her thighs. The ceiling fan above seemed obnoxiously loud in the still room and grated on her nerves. She turned around and pulled down a blade from the blinds to peek out the window.

Damn it. What the hell is taking so long?

She got up from the couch and walked over to the matching chair and plopped down into the big comfy cushions.

This is a bad idea. I just need to call them back and tell them it was all a mistake.

Liz jumped up from the chair, walked into the dining room, and retrieved her phone from the kitchen table.

The chime of the doorbell echoed throughout the house.

"Shit!" She jumped at the sudden intrusion of sound. *Damn it. I need a cigarette and I don't even smoke.*

Liz hurried to the front door and swung it open. She let out a sigh of relief when she realized it was a female deputy.

"Elizabeth Ruiz?"

"Yes, I'm Liz."

"I'm Deputy Chris Parker with the Hillsborough County Sheriff's office. May I come in?"

"Yes, of course. Please come in." Liz stepped back and allowed Deputy Parker to enter before closing the door behind her. "May I offer you something to drink?"

"No, thank you. I'm fine." Chris turned around to face Liz. "I just need somewhere we can sit down and have a conversation."

"Of course, have a seat." Liz pointed to the couch.

Deputy Parker fished her notepad and pen from her shirt pocket as she made her way into the living room and took a seat. "So, Miss Ruiz, how can I help you?"

Liz sat on the loveseat across from the deputy. "Well, I uh..." She scratched the top of her left forearm. "I think I've made a mistake and wasted your time." She stood up and walked to the front door. "I'm sorry."

Deputy Parker settled back into the couch cushion and placed her tablet on the seat beside her. Her voice was soft when she spoke. "Liz, is it?" She waited until Liz nodded her head before she continued. "Dispatch sent me out here to take your statement about an assault." She placed her pen on top of the tablet on the couch. "You and I at least need to have a conversation before I can leave."

Liz slowly walked back over to the loveseat and sat down.

"How about I leave my notepad and pen out of this for a few minutes and just ask you a couple of questions. Would that be okay?"

Liz continued to stare at the fingernail she was picking at but nodded her head.

"Okay, good." Deputy Parker stood up and crossed the room to have a seat beside Liz. "Were you assaulted, honey?"

Liz slowly nodded her head but refused to look up at the deputy for several long seconds. "Not really...I mean, kind of."

Deputy Parker's eyebrows seemed to grow closer together as she analyzed the contradictions in Liz's answer. She did her best to keep the frustration she felt out of her voice. "Okay, why don't you start at the beginning and tell me what happened. Maybe then we can decide on whether we have an assault or not."

Liz scooted her ass toward the armrest of the loveseat and turned to face Deputy Parker. "There's this guy at my gym...it happened two nights ago."

"What happened two nights ago?"

Liz looked away from Deputy Parker. "He followed me into the shower."

"And what happened after he followed you into the shower?"

Liz continued to look away until she felt the deputy's hand on her back.

"Look," Deputy Parker spoke softly. "I understand that this may be hard for you, but I need for you to tell me everything so I can help you."

"We had sex, okay?" Liz blurted out and startled the deputy. "He followed me and he got in the shower with me and…and he did things to me…things I can't stop thinking about…things I liked."

Deputy Parker watched the rise and fall of Liz's braless breasts and couldn't help but notice the hardened nipples poking through the thin fabric of her sundress. She watched her slowly run her fingers over the bare skin of her leg just beneath the hem of her dress and up to her lower stomach, while she spoke as if in a trance.

"Things I want him to do again."

Liz turned to look at the deputy. "I know that sounds weird, but I can't get him out of my head." Liz reached over and grabbed Deputy Parker's hand. "Can you help me find him?"

"You want me to help you find the man who raped you?" she exclaimed, failing to hide the surprise in her voice. "Are you serious?"

"Yes," Liz pleaded. "And it wasn't rape. I mean, I wasn't serious at first but then….Look, we're both women here. You know that one man who just seems to know what he's doing? Always hits the right spots? The best sex you've ever had in your entire life?" Liz scooted closer to the deputy. "I need to experience that again...I know you know what kind of man I'm talking about."

"Sweetheart." Deputy Parker moved Liz's hand off hers and looked her directly in the eyes. "Let me assure you that I have no clue what you're talking about. I am and always have been a lesbian." She stood up and collected her notepad from the couch. "What I can't understand is why you would want to see him again after he took advantage of you."

Liz looked up at her. "I can't stop craving the way he made me feel."

"So, do you want to press charges or not?" Deputy Parker demanded.

"What? God, no." Liz stood up to face the deputy. "I just really need your help finding out where he is. Like an address or something."

Deputy Parker didn't even try to hide the look of disgust on her face as she headed toward the door. "I think you've wasted enough of my time today, Miss Ruiz. If you decide you actually want to report a crime, you know what to do." She pulled the door open and turned back toward Liz. "I'm going to find this guy and see if he admits to the assault. If he doesn't come clean, I'm going to come back here and arrest you for falsely reporting a crime." She slammed the door behind her and stormed to her cruiser.

***

Tommy arched an eyebrow and stared at the cruiser as it slowly pulled into his driveway. He took another swig from his beer and rested it on the arm of the porch swing next to him. The short brunette who climbed out and headed up the front porch steps wasn't bad looking at all, but she had bad attitude written all over her face. He stopped the swing by planting his feet on the porch and waited for her to speak.

"Are you Thomas Reid?"

Oh shit! She's either a man hater or she's having a real shitty day.

"That's what my mama always said." Tommy smiled. "So, I took her word for it."

Tommy stood and stuck out his hand. "What can I do for you, officer?"

She ignored his hand. "I'm Deputy Chris Parker with the Hillsborough County Sheriff's Office. Is there somewhere we can sit down and talk?"

Tommy kept the smile plastered to his face but the humor drained from his eyes. "Follow me." He opened the front door and stepped inside, motioning for the deputy to enter, then closed the door behind them.

"Where should we sit?" she asked over her shoulder.

"I'm good with standing. Been sitting for the past half an hour." Tommy leaned his back against the front door. "Now, what can I help you with?"

She turned to face him and attempted to stare him down for several seconds before answering him. "I understand you sexually assaulted a woman at your gym two nights ago."

"Well, I think maybe you've misunderstood what it is you think you understand," Tommy stated matter- of-factly.

The redness that flushed her face told Tommy that this woman did not like to be challenged at all.

"Mr. Reid? I visited the gym and I've got you on camera entering the ladies shower room just a few moments after Elizabeth Ruiz and not coming back out for thirty-seven minutes." Her voice was hard and climbing octaves with each syllable. "How do you explain that?"

"Well," Tommy drawled. "I'm sure you have her sitting on top of me on one of the benches in the weight room on camera too."

The shit-eating grin on Tommy's face only infuriated the deputy even more.

"She invited me to join her for a shower, which means I don't have to explain anything."

Deputy Parker fought for control over her emotions as she continued to stare at Tommy. "I suggest you lose your cocky attitude with me and find somewhere to sit down so we can sort this out."

The grin left Tommy's face and he eased off the door as if in slow motion. He took a step toward her and his voice was low and controlled when he spoke. “You should have asked me nicely.”

THE END

About the Author

Jace Stone began writing at a very early age and has never looked back. Whether it's song lyrics, poetry, prose, or novels, words are the foundation on which he is building his life. He loves his son and cherishes the time they spend together. When he isn't writing or hanging out with the coolest kid in the world, you can find him at the gym, staying fit and healthy. You can also find him writing romance and poetry as C.b. Roberts @ facebook.com/authorcbroberts

Made in the USA
Middletown, DE
27 April 2017